KIDS CAN'T STOP READING THE CHOOSE YOUR OWN ADVENTURE® STORIES!

"Choose Your Own Adventure is the best thing that has come along since books themselves."

—Alysha Beyer, age 11

"I didn't read much before, but now I read my Choose Your Own Adventure books almost every night."

—Chris Brogan, age 13

"I love the control I have over what happens next."

—Kosta Efstathiou, age 17

"Choose Your Own Adventure books are so much fun to read and collect—I want them all!"

—Brendan Davin, age 11

And teachers like this series, too:

"We have read and reread, worn thin, loved, loaned, bought for others, and donated to school libraries our Choose Your Own Adventure books."

CHOOSE YOUR OWN ADVENTURE®— AND MAKE READING MORE FUN!

Bantam Books in the Choose Your Own Adventure® series
Ask your bookseller for the books you have missed

THE YOUNG INDIANA JONES CHRONICLES™

SOCCER STAR

BY EDWARD PACKARD

ILLUSTRATED BY TOM LA PADULA

BANTAM BOOKS
NEW YORK · TORONTO · LONDON · SYDNEY · AUCKLAND

RL4, age 10 and up

SOCCER STAR

A Bantam Book/April 1994

CHOOSE YOUR OWN ADVENTURE® is a registered
trademark of Bantam Books,
a division of Bantam Doubleday Dell Publishing Group, Inc.
Registered in U.S. Patent and Trademark Office and elsewhere.

Original conception of Edward Packard

Cover art by Bryce Lee
Interior illustrations by Tom La Padula

ISBN 0-553-56011-5

Published simultaneously in the United States and Canada

Bantam Books are published by Bantam Books, a division of
Bantam Doubleday Dell Publishing Group, Inc. Its trademark,
consisting of the words "Bantam Books" and the portrayal of a
rooster, is Registered in U.S. Patent and Trademark Office and
in other countries. Marca Registrada. Bantam Books, 1540
Broadway, New York, New York 10036.

PRINTED IN THE UNITED STATES OF AMERICA

OPM   0 9 8 7 6 5 4 3 2 1

SOCCER STAR

WARNING!!!

Do not read this book straight through from beginning to end. These pages contain many different adventures you may have when you transfer to one of the hottest soccer schools in the country.

From time to time as you read along, you'll have a chance to make a choice. When you've done so, follow the directions to find out what happens to you next.

On your way to becoming a soccer star you'll have to outwit a karate expert who's out to get you. And you'll have to think fast when the bus carrying your team gets caught in a flash flood. But the most exciting challenge of all will come on the playing field—in the big game, with the score tied, time running out, and the ball coming at you.

Good luck all the way.

You're starting a new school this year because your family has just moved. As you approach Hillsdale Central School, you are struck by the beautiful grounds surrounding it, especially the carefully trimmed playing fields behind the school buildings. GO HILLSDALE banners wave above the bleachers. They remind you that Hillsdale has a reputation for turning out some of the best soccer teams in the state.

At your old school you were considered a pretty good soccer player. You had the feeling you might have become team captain in a few years, and the thought of putting your skills to the test at a place like Hillsdale seems pretty exciting. But you decide that it would be a good idea to scout out the team first.

After school your first day, you wander down to the field to watch a practice game between players from last year's team. They are as good as you have heard. The action is fast and rough. It's obvious this squad would run all over your old team.

You're wondering whether you'd have a chance against this kind of competition when Mike Maynard, a kid you had lunch with earlier, taps your shoulder.

"How ya doing?" he says.

"Hey, Mike," you say, but you're distracted by a small scuffle you see on the field. One player has elbowed another one, hard. "Did you see that?" you say to Mike.

Turn to page 2.

2

He nods. "That's Sean Raynor—the team bully. He likes to make other players think he's going to kick them instead of the ball."

"But no one blew the whistle," you say, surprised.

"It's just a practice game," Mike answers matter-of-factly. "Coach can't see everything."

"I hear he's holding tryouts for the team tomorrow," you say. "I think I'll give it a go."

Mike raises his eyebrows. "No offense meant, but from what you told me at lunch about your old team, you're not ready to play for Hillsdale. Not this year, anyway. This is one of the hottest soccer schools in the country. Why don't you go out for club soccer with me? It's perfect for kids who aren't on the varsity level. We have a lot of fun and we don't have to work our butts off the way they do here."

"I'll think about it," you say. "Guess I've got until tomorrow to decide."

"It's up to you." Mike laughs. "Anyway, see ya." He takes off, leaving you to your thoughts. You look back toward the field where the action is still raging. You'd sure like to be part of a great team, but maybe Mike is right. You might look like a klutz up against players like these. Maybe the club team is where you belong.

If you decide to try out for the varsity team, turn to page 35.

If you decide to play club soccer, turn to page 67.

Before you know it, the afternoon of your departure for the nationals has arrived. You're in for a great time, once the bus ride is over. It's due to be a long trip—through some pretty rugged country—and the weather forecast is for heavy storms most of the way.

This may be one forecast that's right, you think, as you climb aboard the bus with your teammates. It's already started raining, and the sky has gotten quite dark. As the bus winds through the curving mountain roads, the rain comes down even harder. The driver leans forward, trying to see through the sheets of water pelting the windshield.

Two hours later, you've dozed off in your seat at the front when you sense that the bus has stopped. You sit up with a jerk. It's dark outside and still pouring. The driver is backing the bus up for some reason. Bob Thomas, the kid next to you, is peering out the window. You tap his shoulder.

"What's going on? I've been asleep," you say.

"The driver said it was only a mile beyond the bridge up ahead to a restaurant, but the bridge is blocked by police barricades and there's no way to cross it," Bob explains. "The water's really high. They must be afraid it will give way."

Suddenly the bus grinds to a stop. The driver shouts, "Hold tight, everyone!"

"Flash flood!" someone yells from behind you.

Turn to page 63.

4

You're center halfback in the final scrimmage the next day—and not surprised to see Sean Raynor playing the same position on the other side. He glares at you from across the midfield line. But you're not going to let him intimidate you.

Your team kicks off. The center forward rolls the ball off to the wing, who shovels it back to you. You give it a boot to your other wing forward, then take off downfield to receive a return pass.

Sean is all over you. As you're trying to get past, he says, "You're not going anywhere with that."

Keeping an eye on him, you feint with your right foot as if you're going to sweep it to the left, then use your left foot to brush the ball right. Sean is off balance for half a second, enough time for you to streak by.

Another player is coming at you, but now your wing forward is clear. You stop the ball and kick it cleanly into his path. He carries it all the way downfield and shoots. The goalie dives. The ball squeaks by. *Goal!*

Turn to page 15.

6

After the game, the coach reads off the names of the kids who are being kept on the team. You're not called. No surprise, you think. Still, you feel awfully disappointed.

As you head for the locker room, Coach Drake jogs up to you. "I watched you carefully during the game," he says. "You're not quite ready to play on the team, but I think you've got a lot of potential. You can run, you've got good ball sense, and you seemed to know where everyone was and which way they were going to move. If you work hard in club play, you should be ready for the team next year."

"Thanks, Coach," you say. Drake's comments restore your confidence, and even though you've been cut, you go home that night feeling happy.

Turn to page 67.

Back at Hillsdale, school really does seem a lot more fun. The reason is that, as Mr. Charbonneau taught you, the more you know about something the more interesting it becomes. Summer school has also made you more efficient: you're able to get your homework done *and* spend a lot of time playing soccer.

You're not sure that you're going to be a soccer superstar, but you're good enough to be elected captain of the team. Your grades are also better than you ever dreamed they could be. So it's not surprising that you have already received four offers of college scholarships. You'll have to decide which one to choose. That will be the most fun of any problem you've had.

The End

8

It's almost dawn when you see a flashing light out the window. A searchlight flickers around the bus. In its glare you see a mud-splattered police car pulling up across the bank. A few moments later you hear an officer's voice on the bullhorn.

"Hang tight in your seats, everyone. Don't move. Rescue equipment is on the way. There's no more rain expected, and the river should be just about as high as it's going to get. We'll have you out of there in a couple of hours."

By the time the rising sun peaks through a gap in the mountains, another police car and a fire truck arrive. The rescue workers swing a ladder into place and drop a rope and harness down through the emergency exit. One by one you're all pulled safely out of the bus.

Half an hour later another bus, ordered by the police, arrives, and you all load onto it. It's heading directly back to Hillsdale. No one's in shape to play soccer for a while, but you don't mind that much—you're just glad to be alive.

The End

10

Your leg comes around in a few days, and with Sean under suspension, there's no doubt about your place on the team. Coach Drake still hasn't announced his starting lineup, but you intend to be in it. Hillsdale's a good bet to win the state championship, and you're not just going to sit by and watch.

You soon learn that halfback is an important position. Being in the middle of the field, you spend more time running than anyone. You're never far from the ball, and there's no letting up.

This kind of running gets you in terrific shape, and all the while you're improving your skills. After a couple of weeks working out with the varsity, you feel as if you're really part of the team.

You're so caught up with soccer that you almost forget about Sean Raynor. Coach Drake sent him to play club soccer, but he doesn't even show up anymore. You hear he's taking karate instead.

Turn to page 20.

A Weston fullback charges you. Even if you get around him, you'll run into a swarm of defenders. Your wing forward is way down in the left corner. You stop the ball and give it a terrific boot right through the defense. Your wing takes it and shovels it to the center forward, who drills it toward the net. The ball rises quickly and even Cliff Lindholm, the great Weston goalie, can't stop it. Score tied, 1–1.

There's not much time to cheer. Coach Drake has warned you about this. "Don't let up after making a score. The other side will take the offense with a vengeance. If you spend time feeling good about yourself, they're likely to score right back."

You shoot a look at the clock—only four minutes left.

A few seconds later you get control of the ball and take it deep into enemy territory. A Weston halfback guards you closely, but you're almost in scoring position. You line up a pass to Mike Kalbacher, your only teammate in the clear. It's got to be just right.

The halfback guarding you sees you're going to pass and cautiously begins moving to block it. Maybe you should fake the pass and try to get around him, giving you a clear path to the goal.

If you pass,
turn to page 36.

If you fake, then take the ball down
to try to score, turn to page 51.

One day you discover that someone on the team really must know who you are. You find a large note, written in black ink, taped to your locker. It reads

VARSITY SOCCER IS NO GAME.
BEWARE WIMP!

You don't know who would have left you such a note or why. Maybe the players aren't as happy to have you as you thought.

Just then, Mike strolls up behind you. He notices the startled expression on your face. "What's wrong?" he asks. You show him the note.

"Who needs those guys anyway," he says. "Why don't you forget about soccer and come with me to Daredevil Park on Friday?"

Daredevil Park, the wildest amusement park in the country, is only about forty miles from Hillsdale. You'd heard it had been shut down because of safety problems.

"It's closed," you tell Mike.

"Oh no it's not," Mike says. "They got things fixed and they're reopening it next week. They're having a preview on Friday for a limited number of people. My uncle Carl knows the owner and he got me a couple of free tickets for their great new attraction—Twenty Thousand Leagues under the Sea. It's supposed to be out of this world!"

Turn to page 14.

"Sounds fun, Mike," you say. "I'll let you know."

Mike nods and walks off, leaving you with a tough decision. Between threatening notes and grueling workouts, soccer has become more than just a hobby. You really could use a break. But if you skip practice, not only will you lose your shot at becoming a star, you'll probably gain the reputation of being a chicken.

If you decide to ignore the note and play soccer Friday, turn to page 33.

If you go to Daredevil Park, turn to page 79.

I might just make the starting team after all, you think. But a few moments later an opponent zips past you and drives on to score.

After the next kickoff the action heats up. Sean, dribbling the ball, is coming at you. You're determined not to let him past. As you force him to the sideline, he boots the ball off to the side, hoping his wing will trap it. The kick is a little wide. His wing hustles after it. Your right halfback is racing him to it.

Smack!

Turn to page 38.

16

Camp continues for eight weeks, and as the final week approaches, Coach Williams makes a surprise announcement. The last day will feature a big game, pitting two teams made up of players from the camp.

Players are assigned by lot to one of two teams: the Buffs (short for Buffalos) and the Bears. You'll be on the Buffs. Your excitement builds the day before the game when Zeke Chandler, an assistant coach at the camp and the Buffs' head coach, tells you that you'll be in the starting lineup.

Turn to page 98.

You decide to ignore Sean's trick and stay in the game. You're not a quitter or a squealer. But your leg hurts every time you put weight on it. You keep playing but definitely not very well.

Later in the game there's a loose ball near you. You'd normally have no trouble getting it, but now an opponent gets there first. He hooks it off to a teammate, who volleys it back. The two of them charge the goal, shoveling the ball back and forth between them. You hobble after them, but your attempt to catch up is futile. Your fullback struggles to stop them, but he can't be in two places at once. A moment later one of them scores on a wide-open shot.

Before the next kickoff the coach calls for time. "You looked as if you were limping," he says to you.

"I got kicked," you respond.

He takes a look. "Put some ice on it," he says, gesturing toward the sidelines. You hobble off the field and have to watch the rest of the game sitting on the bench. The halfback who replaced you isn't that great. Sean Raynor consistently gets by him, which only makes you feel worse.

Turn to page 80.

18

Suddenly the bus slips even more. The driver spins around with a frightened look.

You glance toward the rear. Coach Drake is beginning to make his way up the aisle. He obviously wants to see for himself what's going on.

Again the bus is jolted. You jump from your seat, race to the open door, and peer into the darkness. The water rushing by is at least two feet deep. At the rear of the bus it's deeper. The rain is easing up, but you still can't see much.

"Hey, you in the doorway. Get back in your seat," the driver yells.

You are about to move back to your seat when the bus lurches again. You'd be safer sitting down, but you've got a sinking feeling that at any second the bus could slide backward into the raging river. This may be your only chance to get out and look for help.

*If you jump out,
turn to page 68.*

*If you go back to your seat,
turn to page 104.*

20

One day after a late practice you're walking home alone. It's getting dark, and you are running over plays in your head. So when you round a corner, you're shocked to see Sean there, leaning against a wall as if he's been expecting you.

"How you doing, Sean?" you say.

He spits on the ground near you. There is a gleam in his eye as if he's been waiting for this meeting.

You keep walking. When you're a few yards away from him, he jumps out, blocking your path.

"I told you you'd be sorry for what you did," he says.

Turn to page 40.

"I'd love to, Coach," you say excitedly. "I hope I've got what it takes."

Coach Drake smiles. "Just keep working hard and you'll do fine. I'll expect you at practice one week from today, 3:00 P.M. sharp." He gives you a hard slap on the back and then strides off toward the locker room.

Wow, this is amazing. You are going to be a soccer star for a powerhouse like Hillsdale. You imagine yourself in a crisp new uniform, streaking down the field with the ball on your foot and the roar of the Hillsdale fans ringing in your ears. Next week can't come soon enough!

In the days that follow, you run extra hard to get in shape. During club games you really throw yourself into the action. You've got to be ready for your first varsity team practice. You're not worried, though, because all this additional training has you feeling stronger already.

You wonder what the varsity players are like, since you've never met any of them. During school you notice several team members walking through the halls together or hanging around the cafeteria. They're not loud or obnoxious. Instead they seem to be cool, confident, and proud. They've got the mark of winners, you think.

You're a little nervous about introducing yourself, so you stay quiet. But a few players give you looks as if they know who you are. They'll all know soon enough, you think, when you show them your stuff at practice.

Turn to page 12.

A huge monster is visible, pressed up against the porthole. It's at least fifty feet long, not counting a pair of twenty-foot tentacles that probe the water in front of it, and it looks even more real than the sharks. You realize that this must be the giant squid!

"The titan of the deep," Captain Nemo shouts. As he speaks, the monster veers and lunges toward the ship. "She's furious that we have entered her waters," the captain yells. "Emergency ascent!"

The sub begins to rise, but the next moment it's jolted by a tremendous crash. The entire vessel shudders from the impact. Everyone is laughing, but the laughter suddenly stops. Cracks have opened up. Water is rushing in.

"Emergency. Mayday!" the captain yells into his radio. There is only static in return. Then, without warning, the lights go out. Everything is in darkness, but you can still hear the water gushing into the ship. You can also feel it sloshing around your ankles.

A dim red emergency light flashes on. The water is still pouring in—it's almost up to your knees. In the shadowy light you can make out people clustering around Captain Nemo. He's bent over the master panel, trying to get the controls to work.

If this is a Daredevil Park trick, you think, it sure is a good one!

Turn to page 115.

"I'm Captain Nemo," the man announces. "Welcome aboard!"

The man who is obviously a Daredevil Park employee, has an old-fashioned naval uniform and a long, gray beard, as if he had just walked out of the nineteenth century.

The interior of the sub is also old-fashioned, decorated with ornate seats and carpets made of maroon velvet. At the control station is an impressive brass periscope and a complex array of meters, dials, and levers for maneuvering the craft.

"Take a seat, everyone, and fasten your safety belts," Captain Nemo orders. "Stand by to dive."

Turn to page 32.

You refuse to back down. "Get out of my way, Sean!"

Instead of moving aside, he takes a karate stance. "Not until you get what's coming to you."

"I've got nothing coming, Sean. You started this whole thing. What did you expect me to do?" you ask.

"Not rat on me to the coach," he snaps.

"Rats kick, people talk," you say. Sean glares at you with hate in his eyes. Suddenly he lunges at you.

You step neatly aside and dart past him. He recovers quickly and leaps at you again.

Sean looks meaner than ever. You don't like fighting, but in this case it may be the only way to protect yourself. Then again, you don't want to risk an injury during the soccer season. Maybe you should just run away.

*If you decide to fight Sean,
turn to page 109.*

*If you decide to run away,
turn to page 94.*

Ms. Manley calls an ambulance from a nearby telephone. It arrives soon and transports you to a hospital for X rays. The diagnosis is a fractured leg.

The next day Coach Drake comes to visit you.

"Tough break," he says. "The doctor tells me you'll be good as new but that it will take a few months. I'm afraid you're out for the season."

"That's the way it goes," you say. "Maybe Sean will lay off me now."

The coach asks you what happened, and you tell him all about the fight.

Turn to page 118.

28

"Sorry, Coach," you say, "but I think I'd like to keep playing for the club team."

Coach Drake looks surprised. Then he seems to understand. "Something else catch your fancy?"

"Like another sport?" you ask.

"Another sport, or science, or music—anything that excites you," he answers.

"Nothing special really," you reply.

"Well, soccer is special to me. I have to admit I'm fanatic about it," he says. "But there's no reason it has to be special for you. The main thing is to find something that is, then really get into it. It makes life a lot more interesting." The coach grins, waves good-bye, and is on his way.

As you're walking back to the gym, you bump into Mike.

"Hey, what did the coach say to you?" he asks. "Is he going to make you a soccer star?"

You shake your head. "I think I'll be another kind of star."

"What kind?" Mike asks.

"Don't know yet," you say. "You'll just have to wait and see."

The End

It's not until the next morning that you find out the truth. A headline in the Hillsdale paper reads:

TWELVE PEOPLE ALMOST DROWN ON SUBMARINE RIDE! OFFICIALS CLOSE DAREDEVIL PARK AGAIN.

A couple of days later you and Mike each receive a thousand-dollar check from Daredevil Park to compensate for your "inconvenience and anguish." With it comes a T-shirt that says, *I survived the submarine ride at Daredevil Park.*

Naturally everyone at school wants to hear about what happened. You and Mike are the center of attention. There's not much hope of your becoming a soccer star anymore, but at least you've become famous at Hillsdale Central School.

The End

"Friends?" you ask, holding out your hand.

It takes a moment, but Sean shakes your hand. He squeezes it really tight, as if trying to crush it, but he's not that strong. When he sees he can't hurt your hand, he gives a little grunt, turns, and walks off.

On the way home, you wonder how Sean will act next time he sees you. To your surprise, the next day he shows up at practice. Word around the locker room is that he apologized to Coach Drake and has been allowed back on the team. You expect that he'll be trying to reclaim the center halfback position, but the coach decides to try him as goalie. He tells you to try to kick balls into the goal while Sean defends.

Finally a chance for revenge, you tell yourself, and you shoot with all the strength you can muster. You score a few times, but Sean blocks you a lot.

After practice, Coach Drake gets the two of you together. "I never saw two players work so hard," he says. "You would have thought it was the tryout for the World Cup team."

"Thanks, Coach," you both say at the same time.

He claps you each on the shoulder. "I guess this all worked out. If you play as hard against our opponents as you did against each other, both of you are going to be soccer stars."

The End

With that, he closes the hatch to the conning tower and twists the brass wheel attached to seal it tight. Then he turns several of the knobs on the control panel. The engines jump to life with a low, steady hum. The sub tilts forward.

You feel the craft begin to dive. Then you squirm around to peer through the thick glass portholes on either side of the compartment. You see the water level coming up and bubbles rising. Soon the sub is completely submerged.

"How deep are we going, Captain?" someone asks.

He turns and flashes a strange grin. "To the abyssal deep—in search of the giant squid."

You, Mike, and your fellow passengers exchange curious glances. This Captain Nemo is really into the spirit of the ride.

"He's a real ham," Mike says. "But I'm afraid this ride is going to be a pretty tame one after all."

So far it seems that way, yet you wonder. You've heard that *nothing* is tame at Daredevil Park.

Turn to page 42.

It's going to take more than threats to keep you from playing. On Friday, you show up for practice with the varsity team and throw yourself right into the workout.

The coach has everyone practice dribbling the ball past a couple of defenders while he yells instructions from the sidelines.

"Eyes up. Keep your body between the ball and the defender. Use your shoulder, side, or rump to block his way."

Just before it's your turn, Coach Drake lays a hand on your shoulder and gives you some advice. "Want to get past him? Jerk your head left to make him think you're going left. At the moment he commits himself, cut right. Keep eye contact with him. It makes the fake more convincing. Or if he comes at you at an angle from the right, try moving sharp right yourself. He'll have to practically stop to change direction."

You try to put what the coach has told you to work on the field. You get the ball past the first defender but lose it to the second one. Next you practice the give-and-go with another player, moving pretty far up the field before you lose the ball. You're not the best, but you're doing pretty well. That's what the coach thinks, too, because he comes up and pats you on the back.

Turn to page 53.

The next day you show up at the varsity team tryouts. Coach Drake, a short, muscular man with darting black eyes, instructs everyone to run around the field three times to warm up. Then he leads you in what he calls "body building" exercises—jumping jacks, push-ups, sit-ups, duck walks—each more exhausting than the last. The workout continues until you feel like quitting for the day. But it's just the beginning. Drake barks for attention and lines you up like a platoon of soldiers.

"I'm going to divide you into practice teams," he says. "If you've played a position in the past, you can stick to it or try a new one. For those of you here for the first time, keep this in mind before deciding what to play. If you want to be a forward, you need to be a really good sprinter. You've got to be aggressive and have the agility to score. Halfbacks have to be complete players and need tremendous endurance. They do more running than anyone. Fullbacks should be strong and tough, determined never to let the ball between them and the goal. Anyone who wants to be goalie may have to be the best of all. You need quick eyes, hands, and feet and even quicker instincts."

All at once, everyone shouts out what they want to play. The coach assigns positions, sometimes as requested and sometimes where he thinks best. He looks you up and down and assigns you to play center halfback.

Turn to page 62.

You decide your wing has a better shot. You kick cleanly, straight to Kalbacher. He tries to trap the ball but it bounces off his knee. A Weston halfback darts in and, with a tremendous burst of speed, heads toward your goal. You chase him frantically, stretching at the last moment in a desperate attempt to knock the ball away. You come up inches short. The Weston player lifts a shot over your body and past your goalie's outstretched hands. Weston leads 2–1.

"Don't give up," Coach Drake shouts from the sideline. "Other teams lose. We're Hillsdale!"

You play all out, but there just isn't enough time to catch up. When the game ends, you and your teammates congratulate the new state champs and walk despondently off the field. You can't stop thinking about how you missed that last chance to score.

"Don't look so downcast," says the coach. "You played a terrific game."

"I didn't feel so terrific when I muffed that scoring opportunity," you say.

"You mean when you made that pass to the corner instead of taking the ball down to the goal yourself? That was a judgment call. What you did is normally good strategy. Your kick had to be absolutely true to avoid interception, and it was. If Kalbacher had trapped it neatly, he could have set up a score."

"He didn't have much time," you say.

Turn to page 59.

The Bears fight furiously to get back that goal. You feel as if you're running the marathon as you race to stop each attack. The Bears drive deep and shoot. Your goalie makes an unbelievable save. He holds the ball, then punts it up the sideline.

You're there to trap it, along with three Bears. You can't wait for it to hit the ground. You glance around to see who's where and leap, heading the ball to Dave Piper, your wing.

Dave and you move downfield, working a perfect give-and-go. There's only the goalie to beat. You fake another pass to Dave, forcing the goalie to slide toward him. Then you lift the ball soft and easy over his head. It bounces behind him and rolls into the goal: 4–2 Buffs.

That's the way the game ends. You race toward your teammates, whooping with excitement. It's only the camp wrap-up game, but it feels like the World Cup!

On the way back to the locker room, not one but three college scouts stop to congratulate you.

"Don't break a leg, and don't flunk any courses," one of them says, with a grin, "and you'll get a full scholarship to just about any college you want."

The End

Both players collide and fall to the ground. One of them lets out a yelp. Just as the whistle sounds, you feel a sharp blow to your calf—a deliberate kick from Sean! You whirl, but he's already loping toward the fallen players.

"Hey!" you yell, limping after him. But he doesn't look back. You realize that no one has seen what just happened.

One of the players who collided had the wind knocked out of him, and some of the others help him off the field to rest. Otherwise no one is injured. Except *you*. You can still walk and run, but it hurts. You're definitely going to lose some speed.

Go on to the next page.

The referee has given the other side an indirect kick. Everyone is getting into position before play resumes. You jog along, trying to loosen up your calf, angry about the cheap shot. You wonder whether you should alert the coach to what Sean did. You know Sean will say it was just an accident, and there's no way to prove it wasn't. Maybe you should just ignore what happened and continue playing as hard as you can. Or maybe you should give Sean some of his own medicine!

If you alert the coach to Sean's trick, turn to page 56.

If you ignore what happened and stay in the game, turn to page 17.

If you decide to give Sean some of his own medicine, turn to page 114.

Sean waves a menacing fist at you. "What are you going to do now that the coach isn't around?"

His attitude is beginning to bother you. You wonder if you should call his bluff and see how tough he really is. Of course, there are more rational ways of handling his type, too.

If you say "Get out of my way, Sean!", turn to page 25.

If you calmly walk around him, turn to page 69.

If you stop and reason with him, turn to page 76.

Moments later, the sub lurches and begins to tilt even more. The view through the windows grows darker, giving the illusion that the sub is diving very deep, though of course it's not. This isn't the real ocean after all.

"Three hundred meters beneath the surface," Captain Nemo calls out. "We're now below the depth where sunlight penetrates. I'll turn on our floodlights."

The water outside the portholes immediately brightens. Large masses of bubbles float alongside the craft. A pair of sharks swim by. They look remarkably real, but of course they're fake.

"We're still tilted," Mike says. "Guess we're still diving."

"Pretending we're diving," you correct. "That's just a machine making those bubbles."

A school of strangely colored fish swim by. Then a giant octopus gropes at the ship with two of its eight slimy arms. You know it's fake, but you are oohing and aahing right along with all the other passengers.

Suddenly, a sound like ice cracking on a lake reverberates through the craft, startling you for an instant.

"Nothing to be concerned about," Captain Nemo assures you. "That's just the hull adjusting to pressure—we're now fifteen hundred meters below the surface."

Go on to the next page.

Several people, including Mike, chuckle when they hear this.

"I thought this was going to be scary," Mike says. "It's turning out to be a comedy—" He breaks off as the sub unexpectedly levels and turns wildly.

"Look at that," shrieks a woman next to you, pointing with both fear and fascination at the nearest porthole.

You spin around and gasp.

Turn to page 22.

44

A couple of weeks into the club season, you're in the middle of a game when you notice Coach Drake from the varsity team on the sidelines. You're not surprised to see him. You'd heard that he likes to check in to see how the club players are doing.

Shouts from down the field quickly snap your attention back to the action. The ball's coming at you. Instead of waiting for it to arrive, you run to meet it and smoothly trap it.

An opposing player is charging you. Eyes on him, you jerk your head to the left and shift your foot as if you're going to sprint in the same direction. The defensive man changes course to intercept you, but you're too quick. In a split second you switch feet and kick the ball ahead to the right, then explode after it, regaining control before the other player can recover.

You dribble another dozen yards. Two more opponents are barreling toward you, but your left wing forward is free. You drill him a swift pass. The players covering you hesitate. You race between them, straight toward the opponent's goal.

As you run, you watch your wing take the ball down into the corner. Seeing you break clear, he fires it back to you. You trap the ball, stopping it dead. Only the goalie stands between you and scoring.

Turn to page 52.

Coughing and gasping, you try to swim toward the bank. You hit a rock and spin crazily in the torrent. Your head is trapped beneath the surface for several seconds. Then miraculously the current drives you into gentler waters. Through the darkness you can make out the jagged outline of the riverbank several hundred yards away.

Go on to the next page.

You stroke toward the shore, but once again the current catches you, forcing you toward a rock ledge jutting a few inches out of the water. You crawl up on it and collapse, exhausted, with the waves still washing over you. If the river

rises any more, you're finished. You don't have the strength to go on.

Turn to page 102.

You decide not to take the course, and so do about half a dozen others. True to his word, Dr. Edelman doesn't seem at all bothered. He shakes hands with each of you.

"Be sure to tell your parents that I said they should not be annoyed with you for leaving," he says to the students exiting. "They can call me and I'll tell them the same thing: I think that you're more likely to accomplish something useful if it's something *you* want to do. You may discover that by going home and doing something else for the summer. You wouldn't find it if you were forced to stay here."

Your parents are disappointed when they hear you didn't stick with the program, but when you explain what Dr. Edelman said, they seem to understand.

"Maybe it's not too late for soccer camp," your dad says. He calls Coach Drake and talks with him awhile. When he hangs up he gives you the thumbs-up sign. "There's just one place open, and you've got it. The bus leaves at 8:00 A.M. tomorrow."

"All right!" you exclaim. "Guess I better get my gear together."

The next morning you and six of your pals from the Hillsdale soccer team board the bus for camp. This is going to be a great summer, after all, you think.

Turn to page 60.

Ms. Finley is a middle-aged, dark-haired woman with horn-rimmed eyeglasses. Every time you've seen her she's been wearing a black dress.

When you enter her office, she comes around from her desk and shakes your hand. No surprise, she is wearing a black dress.

"Have a seat. Relax," she says.

"Thanks." You take the chair across from her desk while she returns to her own.

"How are things going?" she asks.

"Okay, I guess," you answer quietly.

Ms. Finley sifts through some papers in a folder. "Coach Drake thinks there's a chance you could become a soccer superstar," she says.

"I play okay," you reply. You're a little embarrassed to hear such praise, especially from the school principal. Besides that, you're wondering what Ms. Finley is leading up to.

"Academically . . ." She pauses a moment, sifting through more papers. "Your teachers say that you have a lot of ability but that you don't seem very involved. What's your feeling about that?"

"Well, I guess I haven't been putting in as much time on homework as I should," you say.

"I'm not going to tell you to work harder," she says.

"Really?" you reply.

Ms. Finley has a twinkle in her eye. She obviously enjoys keeping you guessing. You can't imagine what's coming next.

Turn to page 64.

There's not much time left. You'll have to head for the goal yourself.

You stop and wind up your right leg as if to pass to the left corner. Then you sweep the ball a few yards to the right, speed-dribbling down the field toward the goal. Three Weston players scramble to intercept you, but you're only a few yards away from the goal, approaching it at a forty-five-degree angle. Your fake has given you a clean kick!

Lindholm, the Weston goalie, is positioned a little toward the side you're coming from. He crouches, weight forward, hands up over his knees, palms out, ready for anything.

Now it's your move.

If you aim your kick just inside the nearest post, turn to page 89.

If you try to beat Lindholm with a wide kick just inside the far post, turn to page 58.

If you try to kick over Lindholm's head, turn to page 108.

You see that the goalie has all his weight balanced to one side. With a convincing fake you should be able to beat him the other way.

You feint left, then drill the ball at the net, aiming just inside the far corner. The ball hits the post. FWAP! It ricochets in front of your right wing forward. He rifles it into the net for a score!

Pumped up by the excitement of the scoring drive, you run back for the next kickoff. But a moment later the whistle blows. The game is over, and so is gym period.

Coach Drake is waiting for you by the gymnasium entrance. You'd forgotten he was watching.

"I've had my eye on you," he says cheerfully. "And I like what I see. You're always moving, never letting up. New league rules are allowing me to add a player to my roster. How would you like to work out with the varsity team from now on?"

You bend over to catch your breath and think about this. Getting a chance to play with the varsity is an unbelievable opportunity. But it would involve a lot of hard work, including practicing every day after school. You're really into soccer, but maybe you should continue playing just for fun. That would leave time for you to do other things.

If you tell Coach Drake you'll give the varsity a shot, turn to page 21.

If you decide not to accept Coach Drake's offer, turn to page 28.

"In the final scrimmage game tomorrow, I'm going to put you at halfback," the coach says. "This game is to help me decide who's going to be on the first team, so be ready."

You are jogging back to the gym, thinking about tomorrow's game, when Sean Raynor sneaks up behind you. He lightly punches your shoulder. "Hey, you're quite the coach's favorite, aren't you?" he sneers.

"What do you mean?" you answer.

"Think by kissing up to the coach you're going to beat me out for my position tomorrow?" he says. "You should have paid attention to my warning and stayed away."

"So that note was yours!" you shout. "It figures."

"Remember what I said," he says. "Beware tomorrow." Then he sprints away from you.

You shake your head, wondering why jerks like him exist.

Turn to page 4.

Some kids in the class begin to laugh. The list looks pretty ridiculous:

> NAPOLEON
> GEORGE WASHINGTON
> ABE LINCOLN
> MADONNA
> MICHAEL JORDAN
> MICHAEL JACKSON
> MALCOLM X
> MARTIN LUTHER KING
> JULIUS CAESAR
> HILLARY CLINTON

"Don't laugh," Mr. Charbonneau says. "This is an excellent list. With these people we can trace much of the history of the world!"

You blink when you hear him say that. The list leaves so many important people out. And Madonna next to Abe Lincoln? That's crazy.

"Now, before we continue," Mr. Charbonneau says, "I want you to know that we have a rule here at the Summer Discovery Center. If you lose interest at any time, feel free to walk out of the classroom. Instead of sitting here, you can read, watch television in the lounge, or go swimming in the pond. You don't even have to excuse yourself from class. And don't feel it will go against you if you leave. That's our special rule, and we expect you to follow it. Everyone understand?"

Turn to page 99.

Still limping a little, you make your way over to the coach.

"What's up?" Drake asks.

"While everyone was distracted by the collision, Sean kicked me in the calf," you say.

The coach seems annoyed. "Sean!" he calls, signaling him to the sidelines.

Sean jogs over. "Yeah, Coach."

"What's this about you kicking another player?" Drake demands.

Sean looks at you, hatred in his eyes. "It was an accident."

"Sure," you say. "The ball was twenty yards away."

"Give it to me straight, Sean," the coach says.

"It was just a tap," he says.

"You were trying to hurt me." You bend your leg to show the mark.

Turn to page 100.

"I can't do anything myself," he says. "I was driving along when a rockslide tumbled down right in front of me. A boulder landed under my left front wheel and I hit it hard. It put me into a skid and knocked my axle out of line."

As he's talking he picks up a cellular phone. "I called the police a while ago," he continues. "They said they've got so many emergencies they can't do anything for me until tomorrow. But a busload of kids hanging over a river—they'll get on that in a hurry!"

The driver reaches the police and gives them the urgent message and your location. Within an hour two police cars and a fire engine arrive. The driver stays in his truck. You ride in the police car to direct the emergency crew to the bridge.

The bus is still hanging over the river's edge when you reach the scene. A police officer trains a spotlight on it, and you can see your friends' frightened faces in the windows. The firemen raise a ladder up to the front door. Within fifteen minutes they have everyone safely out.

You get a hug from each teammate.

"Coach," someone says, "think we can still make the game?"

"I like your spirit," Coach Drake says. "But it's three o'clock in the morning. It will probably be a couple more hours before we get to bed, and most of our gear is still stuck on the bus. I think we're going to have a championship team, all right . . . but next year."

Turn to page 96.

It's a difficult angle, but you are sure your best shot is to kick wide, aiming for just inside the far post.

You kick the ball, directing it a little to the left of the goalie. It whizzes by him, glances off the crossbar, and bounces out-of-bounds.

Lindholm has a goal kick. He boots it far downfield, where a Weston halfback receives it. He dribbles several yards, then passes to a forward. The Hillsdale defenders converge on him, but with some quick footwork, he wriggles his way free, shoots, and scores! All before you can get into the action.

It's a goal your team isn't able to win back. In a few minutes, the final whistle sounds. It's Weston's game—2–1.

On the bus back to Hillsdale, you ponder your future as a soccer player. Coach Drake told you that you had what it took to become a star. But your performance this afternoon makes you wonder. Maybe all the coach's praise was just pep-talk stuff. You're a good player, you're sure of that. But that's probably all. You wonder whether you'll even go out for soccer next year.

At least you've got a while to think about it.

The End

"That's right," the coach answers. "He was rushed and had his eyes on the fullback charging him instead of on the ball. That's one reason your pass was not the best percentage play. It's great to be a team player and not hog the ball, but when you see that you've got a scoring opportunity, go for that goal."

"Next time I will," you say.

"Good—this is the kind of thing you learn from experience. And one great thing about experience: keep playing and there's a hundred percent chance you'll get it!"

The team begins boarding the bus. Coach Drake gives you a reassuring pat on the shoulder as you climb aboard. You feel a lot better after your talk with him. Next year will be different, you think. Next year you're going to lead Hillsdale to victory!

The End

60

The Garafalo Soccer Camp is the best in the country. It's going to be terrific fun. The camp coach, Pete Williams, is well-known, and the other kids are all great.

Workouts are scheduled for early in the morning before it gets too hot. By 11:00 A.M. you're sweating and soaked through, ladling water over your head to keep cool. But you don't want to stop.

The drills you practice are designed to improve your technique, but you also pick up some great new tricks, including the spectacular *rainbow*. This is the kind of move only a star can make. With the toe of one foot you lift the ball up the heel of the other foot and then lean forward and flip it over your head!

Each day you enjoy soccer camp more and more. Maybe it's because you're learning all the time. Maybe it's because you're free of the pressure you feel during the regular season. Maybe it's because you've got a feeling you're on the way to becoming a superstar.

Turn to page 16.

62

You and the others trot to your positions on the field. Coach Drake roams the sidelines, motioning at different players to move a little one way or another. The equipment manager hands out different-colored jerseys to each side. Your team, the "Reds," is kicking off against the "Blues." You exchange a thumbs-up sign with your teammates.

The whistle blows, and the game is on! Your center forward kicks softly over to the right wing, who shovels it back to you. You kick to the left wing, who has a clear field for about ten yards before the defense rushes up to meet him. Bodies collide, and you realize that varsity soccer here is a much different game than you are used to.

The Blues score first, but then your team rallies back. You're in the middle of the action, hustling all the time, but most of the others are bigger, stronger, and clearly more experienced. You can't believe they're only trying out for the team!

Out of the corner of your eye, you notice Coach Drake watching, just as one of the other players slips by you. He has no expression on his face, but for some reason you feel sure you'll be cut by the end of the day.

Turn to page 6.

A tremendous thumping comes from the back of the bus. You hang on to the seat ahead of you as the bus lurches sideways, then tilts backward. A torrent of water swirls past outside.

"If this gets any deeper, we're in trouble," Bob exclaims.

"Stay in your seats," the driver yells. He gets up, opens the front door, and carefully maneuvers himself so that he can look out.

The kid seated across from the driver is also looking out the door. He calls over to you. "That river is wild! And it's still rising!"

Turn to page 18.

Ms. Finley looks directly at you. "I've found that students rarely do well if they only do something because they're told to. It would be another thing if you worked harder because you wanted to, but obviously you don't want to or you would have already."

"Well, maybe it's just that I got so involved in soccer, books haven't interested me that much lately," you explain.

"Excellent analysis," Ms. Finley says. "But now it's time to think ahead a little. Do you know what you want to do when you finish high school?"

"Go to college," you answer quickly.

"Unless you're already a soccer superstar?"

"Right," you say.

"But you can't count on that, can you?" Ms. Finley asks, raising an eyebrow.

"That's for sure," you say.

Ms. Finley nods. "Look, some people think that I only like book-learning. The fact is I love sports and I think if you want a career as an athlete that's just fine. But what I don't want is for you to limit yourself. You may find a few years from now that even though you're a darn good soccer player, no one's going to pay to watch you play, and that your marks aren't good enough for college admissions directors."

Go on to the next page.

"So I guess I better start working harder," you say.

Ms. Finley's brow wrinkles. She raises a finger. "That won't quite do it. You've got to get interested enough in some area so that you *want* to study it."

"How do I do that?" you ask.

Turn to page 86.

The following Monday you start playing club soccer during gym periods. Your friend Mike introduces you to a new bunch of kids, and you immediately hit it off. It's a lot of fun.

You notice right away that there are two types of players here. Mike and some others are more interested in having a good time than in improving their soccer skills. But there are plenty of serious players, too. They would probably be on the varsity team at most schools and they make sure that the club games are swift and lively. Still, you're able to hold your own.

After the first few games, some of the better players recognize how well you're doing. As you're walking off the field one day, one pats you on the back.

"Nice playing out there," he says. "Keep up the good work."

Getting noticed makes playing soccer even more fun. You really begin to work on your game. You practice dribbling, using both feet to sweep the ball to one side, then to the other, and using head fakes to throw your opponent off stride. Then you practice moving up field, passing and volleying with some of your new friends. You also work on defense and shooting.

After school, you hang around with Mike, doing homework, goofing off, and playing soccer games on your computer at home. You're settling into life at Hillsdale just fine.

Turn to page 44.

You jump. The wet riverbank breaks your fall, but you have to dig your fingers into the gravelly ground to keep from slipping under the bus. You steady yourself on your hands and knees and then, like some primitive animal, claw your way up to the road.

As you reach it, you hear the sound of tearing metal. You wheel around in time to see the bus sliding backward, its front end tilting sixty degrees in the air! You're sure that in another second it will plunge into the raging river and be swept away. Miraculously it comes to a sudden halt as its back end catches on a huge boulder at the river's edge.

You stand shivering in the rain. Thinking of all your teammates trapped on the bus, you have to fight to keep calm. Only you can help them now. But you'll have to do it fast, before the boulder holding the bus gives way or the water rises any higher.

You look around in the darkness. You can't see more than a few feet ahead, and your ears are deafened by the roar of the rushing flood.

Turn to page 111.

You step aside, intending to give Sean a wide berth. But he has other ideas. He lets loose a karate kick at your nearest leg. Luckily, the instincts you've developed playing soccer have quickened your reflexes. You jump clear and keep walking.

"Afraid of me?" he taunts.

You pay no attention, which enrages Sean more.

He runs alongside you. "Hey," he shouts. "You hear what I said to you? Answer me!"

"What did you say—I forgot."

"I said you're afraid of me."

"Oh yeah, I remember now."

"Well, are you?" Sean demands.

"Why ask me? You said I was," you say, continuing to walk away.

Sean makes a throaty, jeering sound. "Jerk," he shouts.

As you keep walking he trails behind you. "You'd better watch out—I'm not through with you."

You never turn around. That's the last you see of Sean Raynor for a while. A few weeks later you hear he has been kicked out of school for starting fights. Too bad, you think. Sean could have been quite a soccer player.

The End

The Bear halfback tries to dribble the ball by you. You stab your foot at the ball, committing yourself a little early. He flicks it to the right with his left foot, and suddenly he's past you—driving down the field! You pour on the speed and catch him, but he's already passed the ball off to a wing forward. You groan, thinking that if they get a goal it will be because you let them through.

Fortunately a Buff fullback charges the Bear controlling the ball. He tries to pass it but hooks it wide and out-of-bounds. Your wing halfback puts the ball in play. He catches your eye and fires a pass. A second later the ball is practically resting on your toe.

You steal a look at the clock, which is running out: one-fifty-six, one-fifty-five . . .

This may be your last chance. You dribble past one defender, then another, moving the ball into Bear territory. Suddenly both Bear fullbacks charge you. You look for possible receivers. Your teammates are either covered or offside.

Go on to the next page.

You could try to dribble around the rushing defensemen, but that's what they're expecting. Maybe you should cross them up with the spectacular trick move you've been practicing—the *rainbow*!

If you try to dribble around the opposing fullbacks, turn to page 82.

If you try the rainbow, turn to page 112.

Dr. Edelman holds up his hands for silence. "Welcome to the Discovery Center," he says. "Those of you who dreaded coming here, put those worries out of your mind. You are going to find that this school is fun. That's guaranteed! If you don't like what we have to offer, then you can drop out and there will be no hard feelings. Our goal here is to have you find your interests and then follow them." Some of the kids who have been sitting tensely in their chairs relax a little.

"Classes will be held for only two hours a day," Edelman continues. "And you can do your homework outdoors if you'd like. We also have a great swimming pond for cooling off when you're ready for it."

The kid on your left grins at you. "This is sounding better and better," he says.

"I promise you," Edelman says, "that this course will be unlike any other you've ever had. Now, those who are interested may sign up here. The others can return home on the bus later today."

Turn to page 90.

Then, amazingly, brilliant light streams in. Instead of swirling water, floodlights show through the hatch!

You scramble up the ladder and survey the scene. The sub has been raised with ropes and pulleys. Workers are pulling it alongside the dock. In a few minutes you and all the passengers are safely out on the shore.

A man in a blue blazer with a Daredevil Park emblem strides over. "Hope all you folks enjoyed your trip under the sea," he says. "It's our most realistic ride."

"What about our wet clothes?" someone yells.

The man laughs. "Hey, don't get angry. This is no firemen's fair you're at—this is Daredevil Park!"

Now you're really confused. Was what happened really part of the ride?

Turn to page 29.

You've decided you've had enough of this stuff, so you get up from your seat and head outside. Mr. Charbonneau doesn't even glance at you as you leave. You watch TV in the lounge for a while. It's completely boring. You head down to the pond, put on your swimsuit, and dive in. In a few minutes some other kids join you. You're not the only one who got bored!

During the next few days you go to some more classes, but you don't sit through many. You're just too restless. After a week, you tell Dr. Edelman that you'll be going home. He wishes you luck.

Back at home, you can't wait for school to start again. You want to get out on the soccer field and boot goals!

Sometimes you think about what Ms. Finley said. You know she'll be disappointed that you quit summer school. Of course, she doesn't know something that you do—that you can become a soccer superstar. And that's just what you're going to do!

The End

You stop and face Sean, hands up, palms outstretched. "I know you're mad I told the coach what you did, but what did you expect me to do? Just let you kick me anytime you wanted?"

"You could have kicked back," Sean says. "You were too chicken to do it."

"If I'd kicked back, what would you have done?" you ask.

Sean's eyes are blazing. "I wouldn't have let you get away with it!"

"So we would have had a fight."

"Yeah, if you hadn't been chicken," he shouts back.

"And we would have both gotten booted off the team."

"Yeah—well, at least it wouldn't have been just me," Sean says, still angry.

"You were only suspended. You could have worked your way back on the team. You still could. But if we'd had a fight in the middle of a game, with two guys down on the field, we'd have been out for good."

"So?" Sean mutters.

"So—after kicking me, there was no way you could avoid being suspended or thrown off for good." You've made your point, but Sean is not buying it. He makes a motion as if he's about to come at you, then stops.

Go on to the next page.

"You were just hurting yourself. Don't you see that?" you ask.

Sean stammers a moment.

"Look, I'm willing to be friends," you say.

Sean half-grins. "You and me friends—that's a good one."

"Well, think about it," you say. "Having good friends is just as important as having good teammates."

Turn to page 30.

A visit to Daredevil Park is exactly what you need to help you take your mind off things.

"I'd love to go," you tell Mike the next day. "Thanks for the invite."

"No problem," he says. "You're not going to regret it."

On Friday, you and Mike are raring to go. You've heard that the rides at Daredevil Park are more extreme than you'll find at any other amusement park. Since the park isn't officially reopened yet, you'll only be able to try Twenty Thousand Leagues under the Sea. But according to Mike's uncle, it's the wildest ride of all.

When you arrive at the park you are led to a special domed building constructed to house the wondrous new attraction. It is the largest structure in the entire park. The inside is eerily dark and almost completely taken up by a huge pond of water. A hulking submarine is tied up to a dock near one of the edges. It's an exact replica of the *Nautilus*, the submarine in the famous book on which the ride is based.

About ten other people with special tickets are waiting to go aboard. You and Mike arrive just in time. The moment you take your places in line, the attendants start letting passengers on.

You follow the others onto the deck, through a hatch in the conning tower, then down a ladder. At the bottom of the ladder you squeeze through a second hatch and into the submarine's main compartment. A man is waiting to greet you.

Turn to page 24.

That night your leg is still hurting. The next day you decide to see the doctor. He says you have a broken blood vessel and that you should have stopped playing immediately after you were kicked. Then comes the bad news. It's going to take three weeks off the field for it to heal.

There goes my chance to become a star this year, you think. Sean is going to get your slot, and your shot at a championship season. But it's too late to complain about him now. The only thing you can do is get better and try even harder next year. You promise to do just that and to be sure not to let anyone get in your way again.

The End

"Still, all was not well," the teacher continues. "Cruel discrimination was often the rule. It took the civil rights movement, led by Martin Luther King, to awaken America to an understanding of what true equality means.

"The years of oppression had left unhealed wounds. The life of Malcolm X gives even deeper meaning to the history of our country. In a different way, so does that of Hillary Clinton. Because she proves, as well as anyone, how important it is to our country that women have rights equal to those of men." He checks off these new names.

"What about Michael Jordan, Michael Jackson, and Madonna?" you ask. "How do they fit in?"

"A very good question," Mr. Charbonneau says. "They are troubadours, minstrels, actors, who perform for us and who mirror our times. Artists and sports figures are part of history, too. The world would be a far less interesting place without them."

Mr. Charbonneau's lecture goes on for a whole hour, but you barely notice the time go by. When he finishes, your head is swimming with ideas.

Each of his classes after that is equally interesting. By the end of summer school you're eager to take all you've learned back to Hillsdale and put it to work in your new classes.

Turn to page 7.

You're confident that you're faster than the defense and decide to dribble around them. You move to the right, fake a pass, hook the ball left, and shoot by the first defender. But the second fullback is quickly on top of you. You try to pass, but the defender blocks it. Bears and Buffs are all over the ball. A Buff shovels it out of the pack, kicking it toward the corner. A Bear takes it off his knee. It bounces ahead of him. He dashes toward the ball, straining to reach it and the wide-open field ahead.

You race at top speed but realize there's only one way to stop him. You slide, baseball style, toeing the ball clear of the attacking player. He lunges for the ball—too late. Your teammate swoops in and gets it under control. By this time you're on your feet and sprinting ahead of him, ready to receive a pass.

Another Bear moves in to cover you. Good, now you're not offside. Your teammate passes. You trap the ball and wheel, dribbling toward the goal. But you're most of the way over toward the sideline and rapidly running out of room.

You are cutting in closer when two Bears suddenly converge on you. You're at an extreme angle to shoot, but there's no one to pass to. You direct a sharp left-footed kick, aiming at the far end of the net. The goalie launches his body completely off the ground, but he can't stop your shot. The ball grazes the net support and careens in for a goal: 3–2 Buffs. Under a minute to play.

Turn to page 37.

84

Slowly you make your way through the darkness to the police barricade in front of the bridge. Two red flashing lights are attached to it. You try to detach one to light your way, but they are firmly bolted on. You pull with all your might. Still the light won't budge.

Rain is pummeling you, and you are chilled to the bone, but you continue on to the bridge. In the eerie flashing light from the barricade you can see waves splashing over the guardrails. The roadway itself is totally underwater. There's no way of telling whether the bridge is still sturdy—you'll just have to risk it.

You start out over the bridge. After only a few steps the water is almost up to your waist. Crashing waves drench your body. You're as soaked as if you were actually in the river!

Another wave smashes you and drives you toward the metal guardrail. With a desperate lunge you reach underwater and grab its edge to keep from going over.

The bridge shudders. Something must have hit it, maybe a big log. With each step you take, you feel the road giving way under your feet. You quicken your pace to get across before the bridge collapses, but it's rapidly falling away from you. Suddenly the whole structure splits, plunging you into the river. The fierce current sweeps you downstream.

Turn to page 45.

You decide to take the course. Most of the other kids do, too. It's only a couple of hours a day, and besides, you have a feeling it's going to be different than regular school.

The first day of class, Mr. Charbonneau, your teacher, arrives in sneakers and tennis shorts. He sits on his desk, his feet dangling over the side, and grins at you as you take your seats.

"Well," he begins, "what are we going to do in this course? How can we possibly decide what famous people, books, and movies to talk about? There are so many."

You can't help smiling, because you were thinking the same thing.

"Well, let's start with people, to make it simple," he says. "Who are the most famous people in history? Does anyone have any ideas? Just speak out. All ideas are good ideas." He takes a piece of chalk and stands at the blackboard, waiting for responses.

"Napoleon," someone says.

"George Washington," you call out. The ideas come thick and fast. Mr. Charbonneau scribbles them on the blackboard in huge letters. It's not long before he has a long list.

Mr. Charbonneau holds up his hands. "That's it, there's no more room. Of course, we've left a lot of people out. Another group would probably have had a very different list. But let's see." He stands back and looks at the board.

Turn to page 55.

"Well, there are a lot of ways," Ms. Finley says seriously. "It's only a month to summer. For some kids it's a time to goof off. I think it would be very bad if that's what you did.

"Some colleagues of mine have started a summer school," she continues. "It's called the Summer Discovery Center. The idea is not so much to cram knowledge into you but to encourage you to explore areas that might interest you and that you can really get excited about."

"I'm really excited about soccer," you say.

"Good. In that case I recommend you go to soccer camp—I'm sure Coach Drake can get you into the best one there is. If you're going to bet on becoming a superstar, then you better really go for it."

"Then again," you say, "I'm not sure all I want to do is be a soccer player."

"That's fine, too. Then maybe you should go to this summer school. Soccer will still be there in the fall. In any case, think about it," she says, stepping out from behind her desk. "Don't just drift."

That night you think about what Ms. Finley has said. It's a long time before you get to sleep, but when you wake up in the morning, one thing is certain: this summer you're going to *do* something!

---

*If you decide to go to soccer camp,
turn to page 60.*

*If you decide to find out more about
summer school, turn to page 110.*

"What?" you ask.

"That you're not a quitter, you're a fighter," he answers. "You aren't content to wait around and let things happen. And most importantly, it tells me you're a pretty tough kid."

"I guess I am," you say.

"I just realized something else," he continues.

"What's that?" you ask.

Coach Drake grins. "Those traits of yours I described. They're just what you need to become a soccer star."

The End

You spot a small seam between the goalie and the near post. You boot the ball hard, aiming for that sliver of open space. The kick is perfect, but Lindholm, anticipating, dives for it. He taps the ball with an outstretched hand just before it crosses the goal line. The ball rolls harmlessly out-of-bounds.

Your team gets a corner kick, but Weston quickly gains control and moves the ball to mid-field. Just before the final whistle, the Weston forwards set up a great play and drive the ball home. Final score is Weston 2, Hillsdale 1.

The season is over. It was a tough game to lose. Still, you have surprisingly good feelings. You played an excellent game. That final shot of yours was as clean and true as you could hope for. You give Lindholm credit for stopping it.

Next year you're going to practice shooting even more, you think. You're going to learn how to get the ball past Lindholm if it's the last thing you do.

The End

You have mixed feelings about what to do. The course sounds pretty exciting, and you're curious about what you might learn. On the other hand, Dr. Edelman said to follow your interest. For you, that's soccer. What's the point of taking part in a class that your heart's not really in, especially one the teacher says you can drop out of at any time?

If you decide to sign up for the course, turn to page 85.

If you decide the course is not for you, turn to page 48.

Despite your coach's pep talk, the second half is almost a repeat of the first. Only, this time it's the Bears who score quickly and your team that strikes right back. Then the defenses on both sides dig in. A couple of times you pass the ball to a forward in good scoring position only to watch the Bears' goalie make a great save. But every time the Bears get near your goal one of your fullbacks manages to intercept the ball and send it the other way.

You are so caught up in the game that you suddenly realize there's under three minutes left to play, and the score is tied 2–2. You can't help wondering what the scouts think of your playing. You've played a good game, but you couldn't say you've been a standout.

You stop thinking about such things in a hurry when a Bear right in front of you receives a pass.

Turn to page 70.

You head off back down the road. You have to grope your way, inch by inch, as you try to follow the pitch-black path. You can't remember a darker night.

Though you can't see the river, you can hear it raging on your left. A steep slope, barely visible, rises on your right. The rain continues to pelt you, and you are soaked through. You wish you could walk faster just to keep warm.

You've covered about half a mile when you see a dim, pulsing light up ahead. That could be help. You slog your way through the mud toward it. A hundred yards farther the road curves. Suddenly, as you round the bend, you see a big truck with its flashers on. The truck is leaning sideways, mostly off the road. Getting closer, you see that the front axle has been knocked askew. A broken boulder lies in front of the truck. The edge of the road is sprinkled with rocks and stones. You jog up to the cab and shout at the high window.

"Who's there?" the driver calls.

"I'm off a charter bus filled with soccer players," you yell. "It's hanging over the edge of the river and we need help—fast!"

"Come up in the cab," the driver orders. "Tell me what happened."

You climb in and give him the details.

Turn to page 57.

Why be proud? you think. It's not worth it. You take off down the street. Sean runs after you but doesn't follow for long. You're in great shape from running so much in soccer practice. He knows he can't catch you.

"Next time," he calls after you, panting.

You feel good about having escaped Sean's attack, but you suspect that your problems with him aren't over. In the weeks ahead, you see him sometimes after school but always manage to keep clear of him. After a while you forget about him completely.

Now you have time to work extra hard on your soccer. By the time the state championship rolls around, Hillsdale has qualified and you're on the starting team.

The opposing team—Weston—has an incredible record. Word is that their goalie, Cliff Lindholm, is as good as any in the country. Only three goals have been scored off him all season.

There's a lot of suspense building up for the game. The winner has a shot at becoming national champion, and that's attracting major attention. Before the game gets underway you hear that there are scouts attending from several big universities, a scout from England, and *two* from Spain!

Turn to page 116.

"Okay, let's start," Mr. Charbonneau says. "Why do I say the history of the world is revealed in this list? Well, let's just go through it. Much of world history has been dominated by strong, ruthless leaders, bent on power. Caesar and Napoleon are two excellent examples—one from the ancient world and one from the beginning of modern Europe." He makes a chalk mark next to these two names.

"The endless cycle of tyranny, war, and repression caused some people to try to think up a better system, to create something else in the world besides one cruel empire after another. Their ideas led to the principle that every person has rights. It was an idea so powerful that it led to the American Revolution, in which George Washington played such an important role." Again he checks off the name.

"The forging of the Constitution of the United States and the union of the separate states was a magnificent achievement. But grave problems still existed, one of which was slavery. Slavery wasn't the only cause of the American Civil War, but it was the most important issue by far. Enter Abe Lincoln. Thank goodness. For it was Lincoln's courage and wisdom that set the country on a more noble course."

Mr. Charbonneau checks off Lincoln on the board. But he's not finished yet.

Turn to page 81.

96

Soccer season is over. During the off-season you work hard at basketball because you want to keep in shape. But for some reason you can't get excited about it. You want to be outdoors and running on the grass of a freshly trimmed soccer field. You look forward to summer, when you should have plenty of time to hone your skills. It sounds like a great plan until, near the end of the school year, you get a message telling you to report to the principal's office.

You don't really know Ms. Finley—she's only been at Hillsdale since the beginning of the spring term. Your mom told you that the school board appointed her principal because Hillsdale was getting too much of a reputation as a sports school. They wanted a strong-minded person in charge, one who was more interested in books than in soccer balls.

When Ms. Finley first spoke at assembly she mentioned that she liked to have conferences with each student in the school. You guess that's why you're there.

Still, you are a little nervous as you wait outside Ms. Finley's office. You've been so absorbed in sports that you haven't been working that hard in some of your courses. A couple of your teachers have noticed. Maybe that's what the principal wants to talk about.

Turn to page 49.

PRINCIPAL

The game is important not just because it's capping off the summer, but because some scouts from top college teams will be there. If you play a great game, they'll keep track of you. This could be your first step toward getting a college scholarship!

Game day dawns hot and steamy. Since the game won't start until 3:00 P.M. it could be the hottest workout of your life.

Coach Chandler advises you and the other Buffs to drink lots of water. "Who wins or loses may depend on who keeps from getting dehydrated," he says.

Fortunately, by the time the game starts, clouds have covered the sky. It may rain, but at least you're not going to get baked out on the field.

As you warm up with a light scrimmage, you glance up at the stands, trying to pick out the scouts from the big colleges. The next thing you know, you crash into another player. He yells at you angrily. Your mistake makes you feel sheepish, and you resolve not to be distracted during the game.

Finally, the whistle blows. Immediately your mind empties of every thought except getting the ball and moving it down the field and into the goal. You and the other Buffs play well together. Your team scores the first goal, but the Bears quickly strike back with one of their own. You see this is going to be a battle.

Turn to page 106.

You nod along with the others. You've never heard of running a class this way, but you like the freedom it gives you. You settle back in your chair as Mr. Charbonneau begins.

IMPORTANT: *If at any time you lose interest in Mr. Charbonneau's lecture, turn immediately to page 75.*

To continue the lecture now, turn to page 95.

100

The coach leans over to take a close look at the bruise. It's beginning to swell. "I'll talk to you later, Sean," he says. "Meanwhile, you're suspended until further notice." Coach Drake turns to you. "You feel able to keep playing?" he asks.

"I think so," you say. "It'll loosen as I play."

"I think you better put some ice on it instead —you've already shown your stuff this afternoon." He turns to summon replacements off the bench.

You begin walking toward the showers, but Sean is not ready to give up.

"You're going to regret this," he grumbles. Then he pokes you with a long, bony finger and stalks off.

Turn to page 10.

102

The next thing you are aware of are large hands lifting you off the rock ledge. A team of men clad in orange storm suits and black hip boots has come to rescue you. They lower you by rope into a bright-yellow inflatable raft. You're too cold and battered to talk to them, but you do notice that the sun is shining and the river has fallen a little. Groggily you realize that your nightmare is over. Then you pass out again.

You wake up in the hospital, sick and aching, but mainly wondering what happened to your teammates. You ask a nurse passing by and learn that they were all rescued shortly after dawn. She also tells you that you are going to be okay. News like that is the best medicine you could have.

The next day Coach Drake visits you. "I was so relieved when I heard you'd been rescued," he says. "We were all worried about you."

You smile when you hear that. "I was afraid everyone might think of me as someone who jumped off the sinking ship."

"Don't worry about it," he says. "You couldn't help the others by staying on the bus. You made a decision, and I respect that. You risked your life to try to get help. If you'd made it to the restaurant, they probably could have gotten rescuers to us several hours earlier. That might have made all the difference. You know what that proves to me?"

Turn to page 88.

"I'm sorry, Coach," you say.

The coach examines your leg, then Sean's. "You're lucky neither of you got seriously hurt," he says. "I'm suspending both of you from the team, but don't leave the field. I want you to sit on the bench and hold some ice to those legs."

He turns to talk to the other players. You and Sean limp off the field.

Sitting on the bench a little later, Sean says, "Do you think the coach will let us back on the team?"

"That's what I was wondering," you say. "I wouldn't blame him if he didn't."

After a while Sean says, "That was pretty dumb of me to kick you."

"It was pretty dumb of me to kick you back," you say.

After practice the coach walks by. Barely turning to look at you, he says, "You're both suspended until the doctor says it's okay for you to play again." He stalks on without waiting to hear what you might say.

Sean lets out a deep breath. "Looks like we have another chance," he says.

You're thinking the same thing, and another thing as well—you're going to beat Sean out for the starting position if you have to practice every day of the week and twice on Sundays.

The End

It's too dangerous outside, you decide. You'd never get more than a few feet away from the bus in the roaring current.

As you start back to your seat, one step at a time, the bus slips again. You are pitched into an empty seat nearby. The bus keeps sliding, headed for the river.

The next sound you hear is a horrific crunching as the bus violently stops short, tilted at a sixty-degree angle. Some of your teammates are pinned in their seats, yelling.

The front headlights beam up toward the sky, illuminating the driving rain. There's still a dim light on inside the bus. You peer over your shoulder. One kid has started climbing over the seat ahead of him.

"Stop!" It's Coach Drake, shouting. "Everyone stay absolutely still!" The bus quiets down instantly. In a milder voice the coach continues. "I think we were held from sliding into the river by a big rock, but we're in a very precarious spot. Just moving around could be enough to jolt us loose."

A lot of kids start whispering nervously.

"It's all right to talk, but keep your voices down," the coach says. "The rains have almost stopped, and I think the worst is over. But I repeat—*don't move*. We'll be rescued in a few hours if we just keep our heads."

Go on to the next page.

There is nothing to do but sit and wait and hope. An hour goes by, then another, and then another. The rain stops but the sheer strength of the flooded river keeps the water climbing. Waves slap against the back of the bus. This is the most frightening thing that has ever happened to you, and your terror is heightened by the fact that you can't do anything about it.

Turn to page 8.

106

You get off some great kicks and headers, and your dribbling is spectacular, even against the Bears' strong, fast players. But the defenses hold tight. The first half ends with the score tied, one all.

Back in the locker room, Zeke huddles the team together. "Coach Williams must be thinking that he matched these teams perfectly," he says. "It's up to us to prove he's wrong. We've got to show that we never ease off, that we keep up the pressure and play hard straight through to the end of the game. We're going to score, score, score. And we're never going to let them through."

You and your teammates let out a cheer, then head back to the field.

Turn to page 91.

Your eyes zero in on the upper corner of the net. You kick the ball, lifting it a little, aiming just over the goalie's head. It flies straight and true. Lindholm makes a terrific leap for it but falls to the ground as the ball zips by. Time seems to stop as you watch it roll down the inside of the net.

A cheer erupts from your teammates. Your goal puts Hillsdale ahead, 2–1—with less than three minutes to play. But Weston is about to kick off, and you know they're determined to score.

Running down the field, you remember things Coach Drake has told you: Don't let down after making a goal. Hustle all the time. Contain your opponents. Never let up the pressure. Don't overcommit.

All the months of practice seem worth it now. You're playing on instinct, running, marking free players, trapping the ball and moving it downfield. There's no way you or the other Hillsdale players are going to give that goal back.

You don't. When the final whistle blows, it's Hillsdale 2, Weston 1. Your team is state champ!

After the game, Coach Drake gathers the sweaty but joyous team around. "Great game, gang!" he shouts. "But this is just the beginning."

You know exactly what he means. Two weeks from now you'll be headed for the biggest game of your life and a shot at the national championship.

Turn to page 3.

You raise your arms to fend off Sean's blow, bracing yourself for a fight. Sean lets loose a karate kick. Again you step aside, but this time your foot lands on some wet leaves. You lose your balance and fall down hard on the concrete. A sharp pain stabs through your back. You can hardly move. Sean stands over you, jeering.

"What a pushover. Didn't even have to touch you." Then he steps back and sees you're really hurting.

A car screeches to a stop alongside you. At the wheel is Ms. Manley, one of your teachers at school. She rolls down the window. "What happened here?" she asks.

"My friend slipped," Sean says.

"Slipped! You liar!" Your outburst causes you to wince with pain before you can explain further.

"It was an accident," Sean says.

Ms. Manley hops out of her car. "Quiet down, both of you," she says. "The most important thing is to make sure you're all right."

Turn to page 27.

110

You could take a chance on becoming a big soccer star, but the odds are against it. There's just too much competition out there. You like Ms. Finley's idea of exploring different areas to find something that really interests you.

The week after school lets out you board a bus for the Summer Discovery Center, the school Ms. Finley recommended. You'll be attending the orientation session, at which you'll get details about the class and have the chance to enroll if it intrigues you.

The Summer Discovery Center is actually at a day school called Oakwood. Oakwood is only twenty miles from Hillsdale, but they never play soccer against you—they're just not good enough. They are pretty good at other things, however. Your parents have checked into Dr. Edelman, the director. By all reports he is a smart and energetic man. The course is also highly rated. It's about history, movies, and books and how they relate to you. But instead of just teaching a lot of facts, the course is supposed to really involve students in what's going on in the world.

Soon after you arrive, you and the other fifty-eight summer students are called into the assembly room. Dr. Edelman, looking younger than you had expected, is already onstage. You wonder if *he* would rather be in soccer camp by the way he keeps pacing back and forth on the stage. The room is hot and stuffy, and you're beginning to wish you hadn't come.

Turn to page 72.

Then, just up ahead, you see the flashing red lights of the police barricade in front of the bridge. You remember that only a mile farther on there should be a restaurant where you may be able to find help. The bridge is closed—and almost completely submerged—but somehow you might be able to get across it.

Your alternative is to run back down the road the way you came and try to flag down a passing motorist. In this weather it's unlikely many people are out driving, but it could be worth a shot. If you're going to save your friends, you'll have to try something.

*If you attempt to cross the bridge,
turn to page 84.*

*If you decide to run back down the road,
turn to page 93.*

You've been waiting for this moment. It's time to show your stuff. It's time for the *rainbow*!

As the Bears close in on you, you work the ball from the toe of your back foot onto the heel of your front foot, then lean forward and flip it deftly over the defenders' heads. You race between them before they can reverse direction. One of them has a startled expression on his face as you go by. He can't believe what's happened!

Now the ball is loose. Your kick sliced more toward the sideline than you intended. A Bear halfback—the fastest man on their team—beats you to the ball and begins racing downfield toward your goal.

Everyone is in motion again, trying to regroup. You glance at the clock: only twenty-two seconds left. It's all over, you think.

But the Bears have not given up. A halfback sends a beautiful pass into the Buff corner, where a forward picks it up. He dribbles it in front of the goalie, then sends a no-look pass to a teammate who boots it in: 3–2 Bears with five seconds to go. It *is* all over now. The Bears have won.

You walk off the field feeling you played a pretty good game. But you notice there aren't any scouts coming over to talk to you.

"Just the same, I'm going to be a soccer star," you tell yourself. Maybe you won't. Maybe you will.

The End

114

You're not going to ignore what happened! Your leg hurts, but you decide to stay in the game and do the best you can. As soon as the ball is downfield, you work your way over to Sean. His eyes are on the ball, and he doesn't see you coming. You give him a swift kick in the same place he got you. He yells and wheels around in pain. The whistle blows. Coach Drake races angrily toward you.

"I saw that!" he yells. "There's not going to be any of that on my team!"

"He started it!" you call to the coach. "He deliberately kicked me first." But the look in Coach Drake's eyes tells you he doesn't care. You have a feeling your Hillsdale soccer career is over.

"Did you start it?" the coach asks Sean.

"Not really," Sean replies.

"Not really? Was it an accident?" the coach asks.

"No way," you say before Sean can respond. "You kicked me after the wings collided and the whistle had blown."

The coach looks hard at Sean. "Is that right?"

Sean mumbles something, refusing to look the coach in the eye.

"I'll take that to mean you did it, Sean," Coach Drake says. Then he turns to you. "But just because he started it doesn't give you the right to kick him back. If I let that go on we'd have a lot of fights instead of soccer games on this field."

Turn to page 103.

"This is no trick," Mike screams, grabbing your arm. "We could drown here. We've got to escape before it's too late!" He leaps up and tries to turn the wheel on the hatch to the conning tower.

You run up to help him.

"Don't!" Captain Nemo bellows. "I've almost got the emergency system working."

"We'll be swimming by then!" someone shouts back.

Mike is having trouble getting the wheel to turn. "Help me!" he yells at you.

With both of you twisting the wheel mightily, the hatch finally swings open. Water gushes in. You struggle to climb through, but a torrent of waves hurls you back.

People behind you are thrashing about in the water. The sub is filling up. There's no other exit. It seems unbelievable that this is happening, but you have a strong feeling that you're about to drown!

Turn to page 74.

116

The championship game is as tough as you expected. You are using the same plays that have worked all season, but you and your teammates can't seem to score. You get the ball to your forwards a good deal, but they can't get past Weston's fullbacks. The few times they get to shoot, they either miss or the goalie makes a remarkable save. Fortunately you are playing great defense too. As the first half comes to a dramatic close, there's no score.

In the second half your team hustles more than ever, holding Weston at bay. Midway through the half one of your forwards gets in great scoring position only to have Lindholm snare the ball with a sensational dive. He immediately punts the ball a fantastic distance, sending it looping all the way downfield. Suddenly all the rest of the Weston team seems to be downfield too, driving through the Hillsdale defense. They overpower your fullback and rocket a shot into the net for a score.

You glance at the clock. Only ten minutes left. Your team has to score, but the Weston players are determined to keep you away from their goal. You keep hustling and finally get a chance. After making a steal at midfield, you dribble around a Weston halfback and move the ball almost to within shooting distance of the goal.

Players from both sides bunch ahead of you.

Turn to page 11.

118

Coach Drake listens, shaking his head. "That Sean Raynor could be a good kid, but he has a tremendous chip on his shoulder. I'm going to try to arrange for him to get counseling. I think it would do him a lot of good."

"And me too," you say.

"I don't think he'll bother you anymore," the coach says. "Once you're mended you've got a clear field ahead. It may take you a year longer to become a soccer star, but I'm convinced it's going to happen."

The End

ABOUT THE AUTHOR

EDWARD PACKARD is a graduate of Princeton University and Columbia Law School. He developed the unique storytelling approach used in the Choose Your Own Adventure series while thinking up stories for his children Caroline, Andrea, and Wells.

ABOUT THE ILLUSTRATOR

TOM LA PADULA graduated from Parsons School of Design with a BFA and earned his MFA from Syracuse University.

For over a decade Tom has illustrated for national and international magazines, advertising agencies, and publishing houses. Besides his illustrating, Tom is on the faculty of Pratt Institute, where he teaches a class in illustration.

During the spring of 1992, his work was exhibited in the group show "The Art of the Baseball Card" at the Baseball Hall of Fame in Cooperstown, New York. In addition, the corporation Johnson & Johnson recently acquired one of Tom's illustrations for their private collection.

Mr. La Padula has illustrated *The Luckiest Day of Your Life, Secret of the Dolphins, Scene of the Crime,* and *The Secret of Mystery Hill* in the Choose Your Own Adventure series. He resides in New Rochelle, New York, with his wife, son, and daughter.